Darcie Tay...

Illustrations By: Kenny Lou...

My Little
RED WAGON

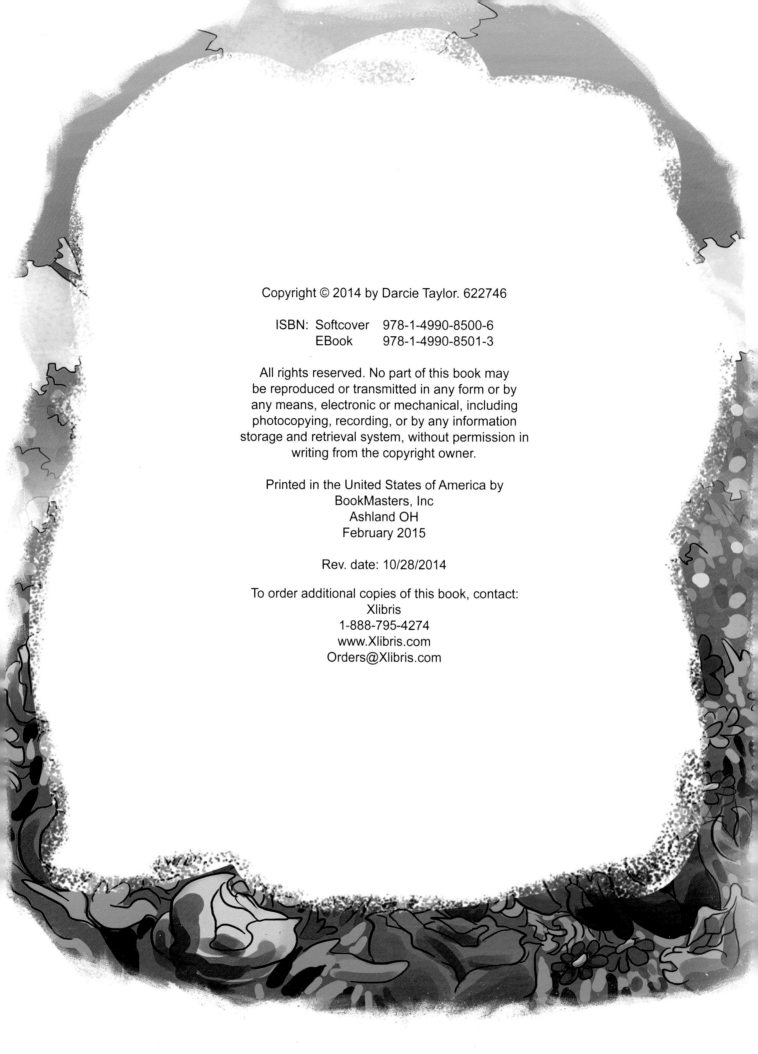

Printed in the United States of America by
BookMasters, Inc
Ashland OH
February 2015

Rev. date: 10/28/2014

To order additional copies of this book, contact:
Xlibris
1-888-795-4274
www.Xlibris.com
Orders@Xlibris.com

My Little
RED
WAGON

Darcie Taylor

Illustrations By: Kenny Estrella

Once upon a time, there was a little girl who loved flowers. She loved red ones, blue ones, yellow ones, pink ones and white ones. Everywhere she went, she would look for flowers.

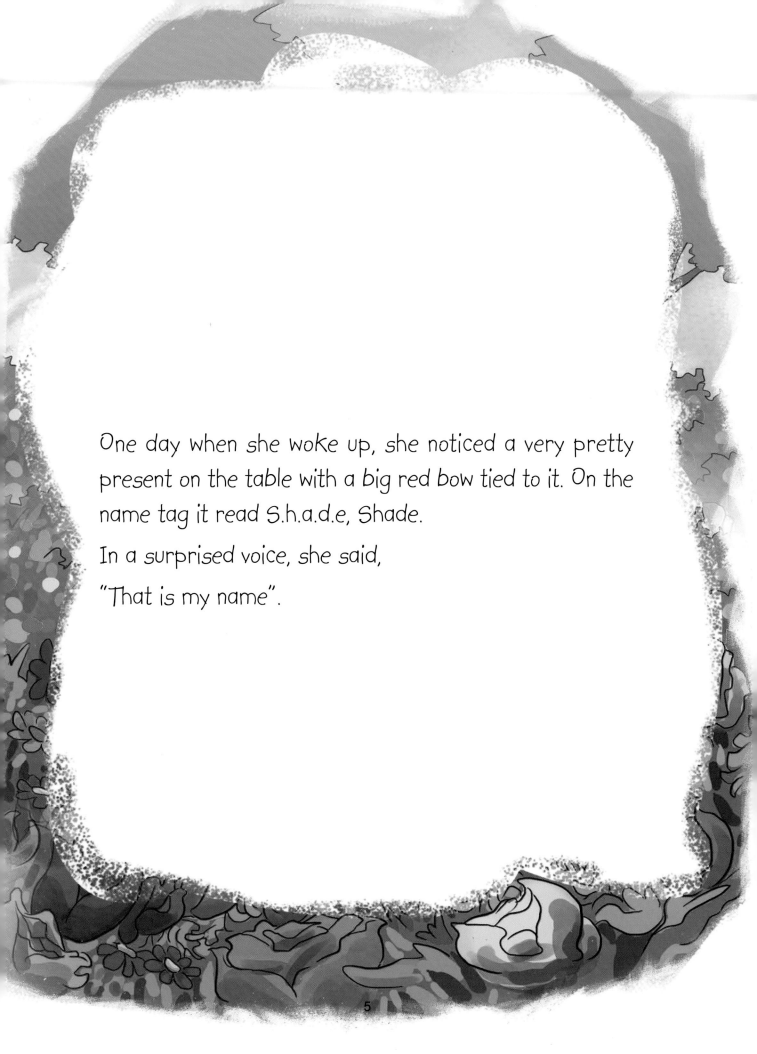

One day when she woke up, she noticed a very pretty present on the table with a big red bow tied to it. On the name tag it read S.h.a.d.e, Shade.

In a surprised voice, she said,

"That is my name".

She thought to herself,

"It isn't Christmas so it's not from Santa Clause. It isn't Easter so it's not from the Easter Bunny, and it isn't my birthday. I wonder who left me this present?"

The little girl went to find her mother, who was working out in her garden.

"Mommy, mommy, there is a present on the table with my name on it. Who is it from, and why do I get a present?"

They went back into the house to get it. As her mom handed her the present, she said,

"It's from me. It's something I hope you will enjoy as much as I do."

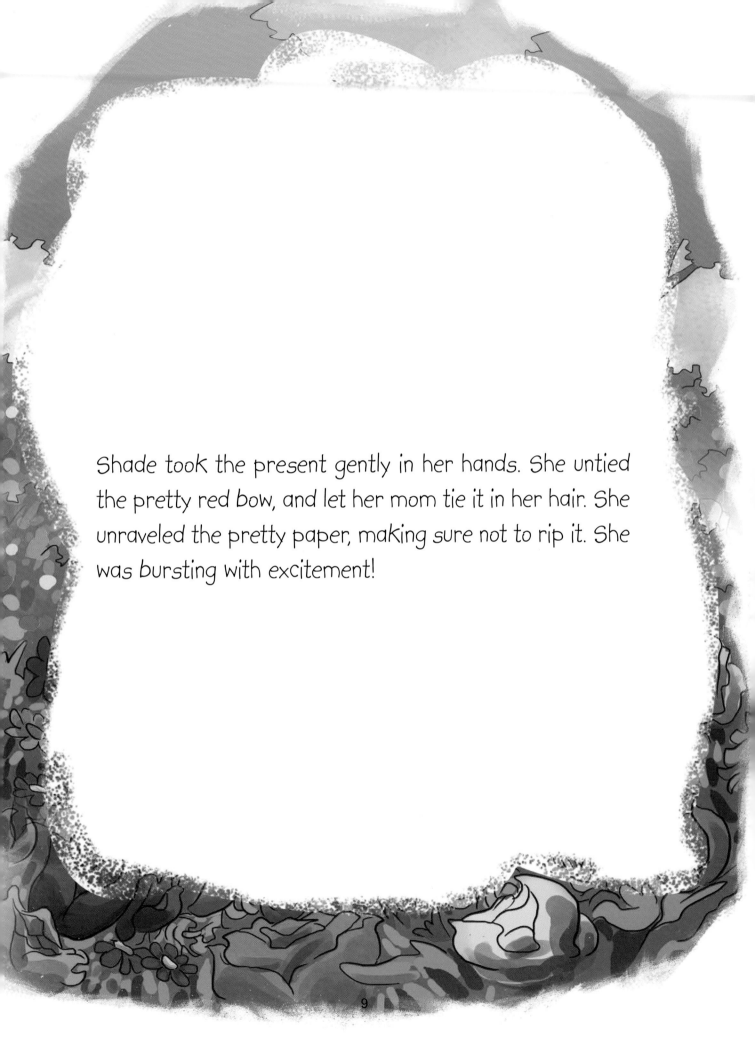

Shade took the present gently in her hands. She untied the pretty red bow, and let her mom tie it in her hair. She unraveled the pretty paper, making sure not to rip it. She was bursting with excitement!

Inside, she found 5 packages of flower seeds. There was a package of red ones, blue ones, yellow ones, pink ones and white ones. All her favorite colors! Shade was so happy that she was going to plant and grow her own flowers, just like her mom.

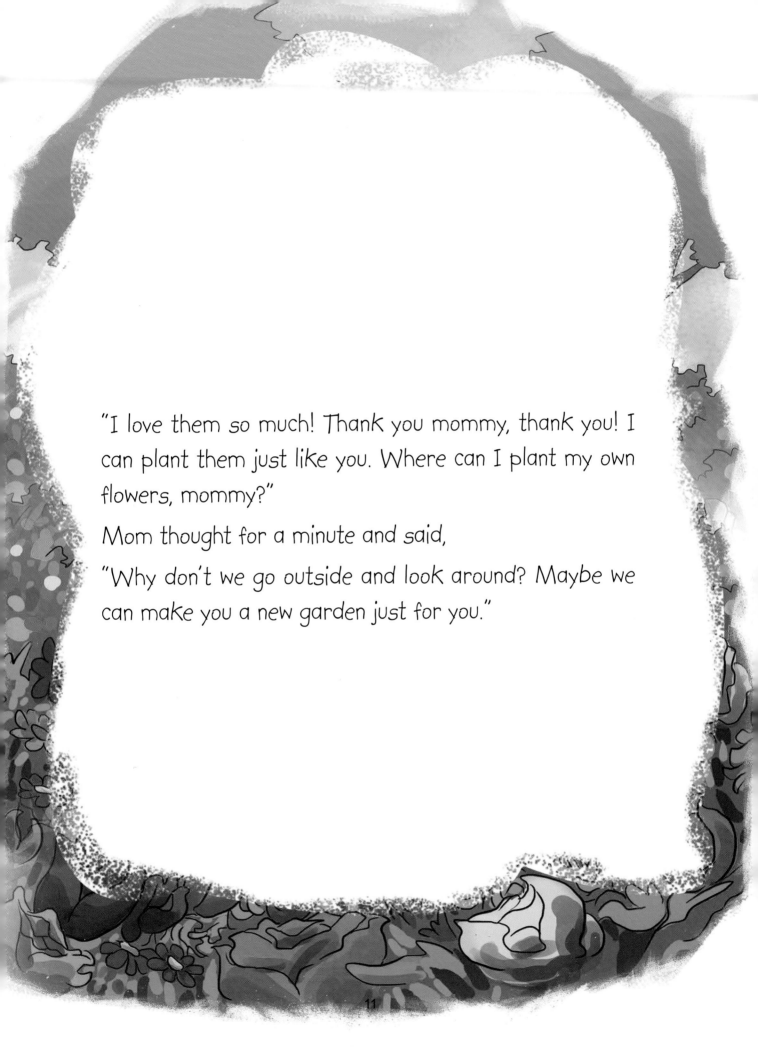

"I love them so much! Thank you mommy, thank you! I can plant them just like you. Where can I plant my own flowers, mommy?"

Mom thought for a minute and said,

"Why don't we go outside and look around? Maybe we can make you a new garden just for you."

Shade and her mom went outside to see where they could create a new garden, just for her. They looked everywhere in the yard. The front yard had many little gardens of flowers already growing. She continued to look in the back yard, but it was filled with patches of flowers and vegetables. She couldn't find a new place for her own garden. Shade sat down on the back step, feeling sad and wondering where she could plant her flowers.

As she looked around her back yard pouting, she noticed her little red wagon beside the fence. She jumped up and ran over to it, tugging and pulling until it came loose from the huge pile of leaves it was sitting in.

"Mommy, mommy, can I plant them in here? Please, please mom?" The little girl screamed with excitement.

Her mom turned to see what she had in mind.

"What a great idea Shade. Let's start by filling it full of black dirt."

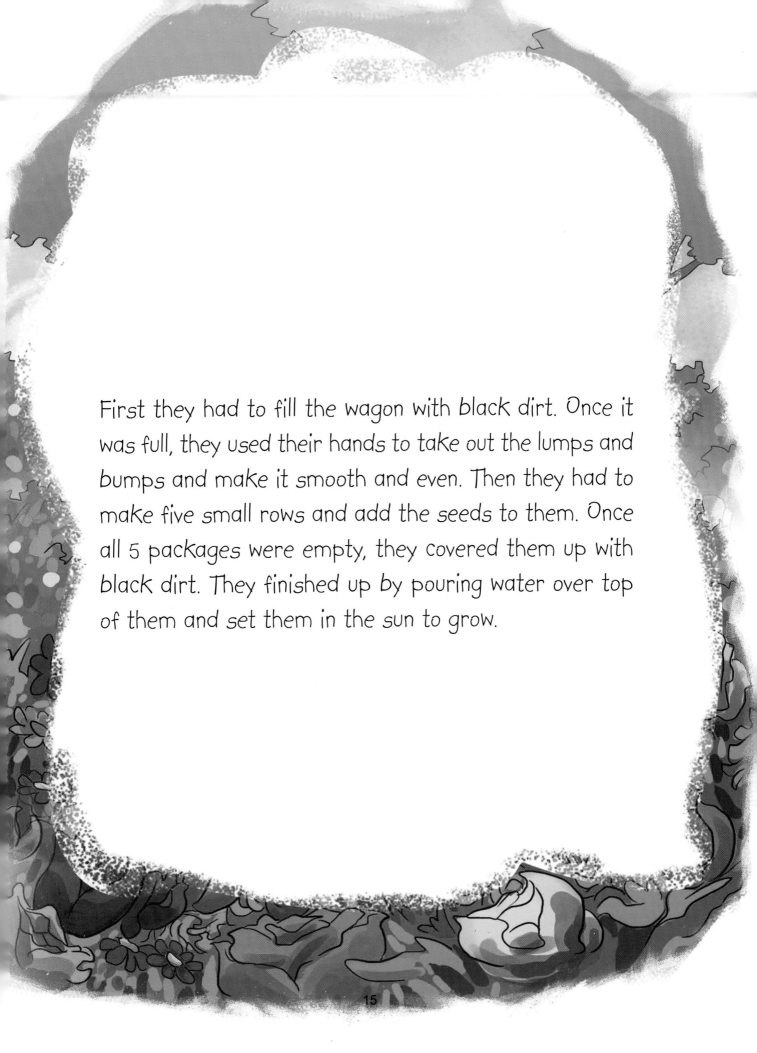

First they had to fill the wagon with black dirt. Once it was full, they used their hands to take out the lumps and bumps and make it smooth and even. Then they had to make five small rows and add the seeds to them. Once all 5 packages were empty, they covered them up with black dirt. They finished up by pouring water over top of them and set them in the sun to grow.

Shade was so happy she was going to have her own flowers to take care of, just like her mom. Each day she would wake up and run outside to see if they were growing. She would make sure to give them plenty of water and push them into the sunshine where they would grow big and strong. She even took them for walks in their little red wagon. They went everywhere with her.

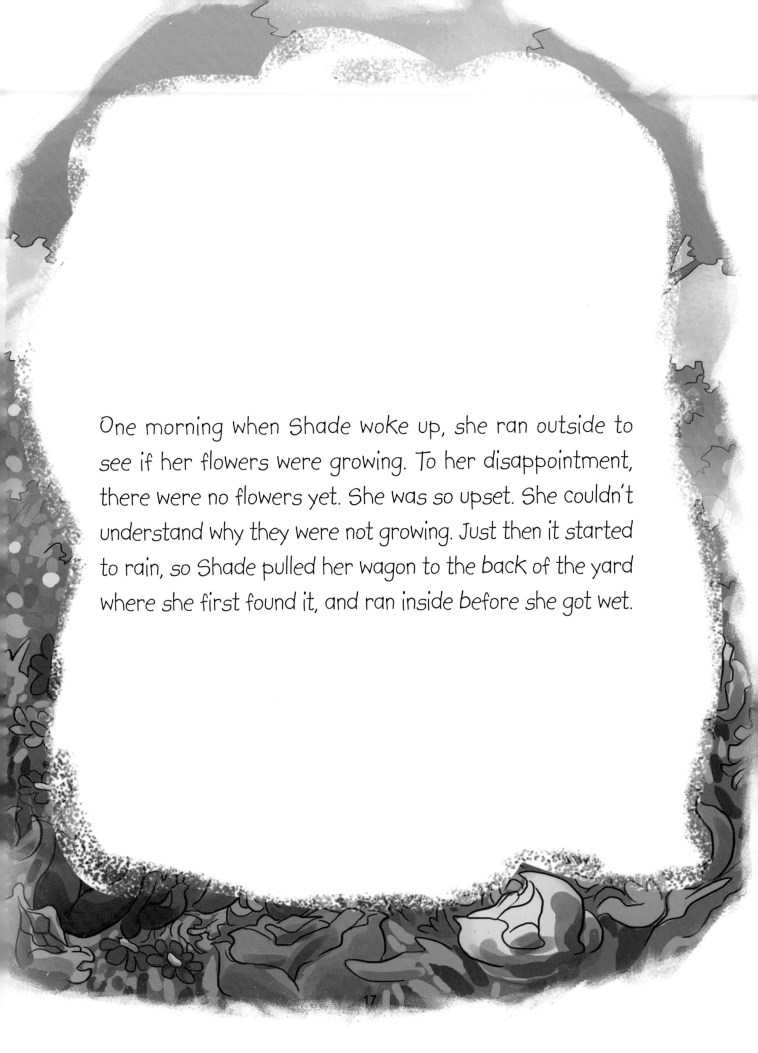

One morning when Shade woke up, she ran outside to see if her flowers were growing. To her disappointment, there were no flowers yet. She was so upset. She couldn't understand why they were not growing. Just then it started to rain, so Shade pulled her wagon to the back of the yard where she first found it, and ran inside before she got wet.

By the afternoon, it was pouring rain. It rained and rained for 3 days. It rained so hard that the little girl was unable to go outside to play. She just stood sadly at the window, staring out towards her wagon.

On the forth morning, Shade's mother woke her up by dancing and singing,

"What a beautiful day, time to get up, up and enjoy the day! Time to get up and play!"

Shade didn't want to tell her mom that her flowers hadn't grown, so she got up, got dressed, and went outside to take her wagon for a walk.

As Shade walked closer and closer to her wagon, she could see that something was growing inside of it. She ran to get a closer look, and couldn't believe her eyes. In five little rows, there were little sprouts of green stems growing. Her eyes grew wide with delight and she couldn't hold back her smile.

She ran back into the house yelling, "Mommy, mommy! Come see, come see!" Shade grabbed her mom's hand and pulled her out the back door. "Mom, look! My flowers are growing! I am growing flowers, just like you!" Her mom laughed at her daughter's excitement. "I knew you could do it! I'm so proud of you!"

21

Every day after that, Shade would water her sprouts, and let them sit in the sun. She would take them everywhere, always singing and dancing as she pulled them along. Day after day her sprouts kept growing and growing. She noticed them getting bigger and bigger.

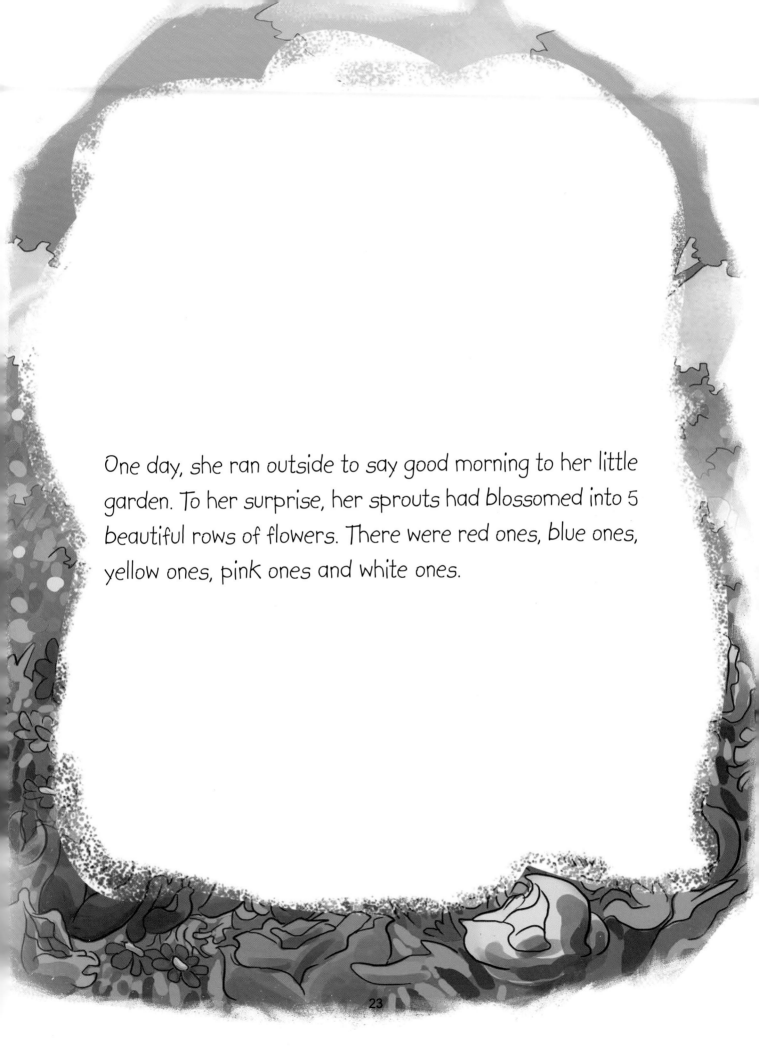

One day, she ran outside to say good morning to her little garden. To her surprise, her sprouts had blossomed into 5 beautiful rows of flowers. There were red ones, blue ones, yellow ones, pink ones and white ones.

She called for her mom. "Mommy, mommy! Come see, come see!"
Her mom came running out. Shade's little red wagon blossomed into
a beautiful little garden. Her heart beamed with joy for her little girl.

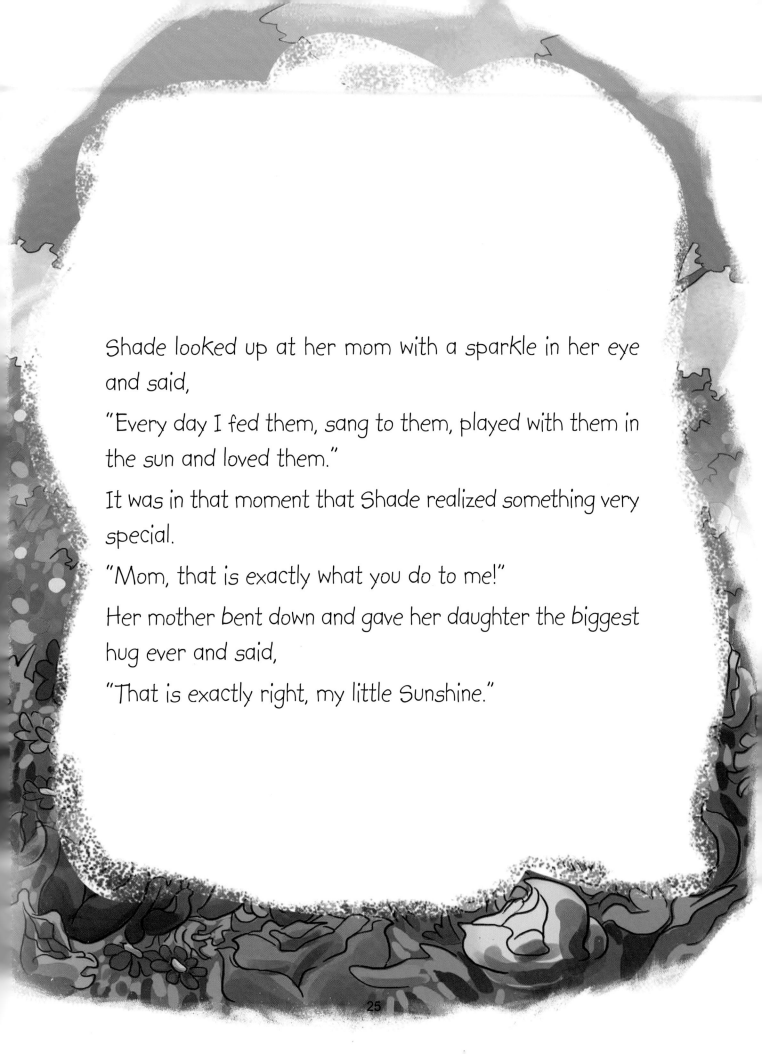

Shade looked up at her mom with a sparkle in her eye and said,

"Every day I fed them, sang to them, played with them in the sun and loved them."

It was in that moment that Shade realized something very special.

"Mom, that is exactly what you do to me!"

Her mother bent down and gave her daughter the biggest hug ever and said,

"That is exactly right, my little Sunshine."

Shade looked up at her mom with a confused look on her face and asked,

"Mommy, how come you just called me Sunshine?"

Her mom smiled and replied,

"Because you can't have Shade without it."

They both laughed and hugged each other tight.

The End